KIVIOK'S MAGIC JOURNEY

AN ESKIMO LEGEND Written and illustrated by

JAMES HOUSTON

A Margaret K. McElderry Book   ATHENEUM 1973 NEW YORK

By the same author

For Young Readers

Akavak
Eagle Mask
Ghost Paddle
Songs of the Dream People
Tikta'liktak
The White Archer
Wolf Run

For Adults

The White Dawn (a novel)
Eskimo Prints
Ojibway Summer

To William and Amanda

KIVIOK'S MAGIC JOURNEY

Have you ever heard of the Eskimo, Kiviok? Have you seen him in your travels? Many wonderful tales are told of Kiviok in all the igloos of the North. It is said that

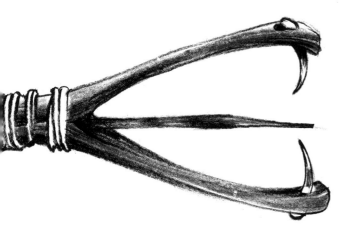

Kiviok first appeared soon after the sun and moon came to light the world. At that time animals could easily turn themselves into humans and humans often turned themselves into animals. It was a time before wolves had learned to hunt the deer, before foxes tried to catch the geese.

One evening in early summer when the north wind stood still and the whole sky blazed red with the rays of the setting sun, Kiviok the Eskimo stepped out of his tent, picked up his fishing spear and walked across the wide lonely plain that led down to the silent lake.

Imagine his surprise when he heard soft laughter and the sound of splashing, and saw six beautiful girls playing in the cold clear water near the shore. So happy were they that they did not see Kiviok. He sat down quietly to watch them.

Suddenly Kiviok saw a wicked raven swoop out of the sky and snatch up one of the white feather coats that the girls had left on the shore.

"*Cawk! Cawk! Cawk!*" The raven laughed, as he rose into the air and flew westward, holding the white feather coat in his beak.

Seeing the raven, the girls rushed in toward the shore.

"*Kungo! Kungo! Kungo!*" they cried in their musical voices, quickly pulling on their downy white coats.

While Kiviok watched, five of the girls turned swiftly into snow geese and rose on wide white wings. Soaring upward into the evening sky, the five snow geese circled the lake, calling, "*Kungo, kungo, kungo,*" to their sister left below.

One remained on the shore, for she could not fly. The raven had stolen her feather coat. She could only stand shivering, calling out to her five sisters in a sad voice, "*Kungo, kungo, kungo, kungo, kungo,*" as she watched them fly away.

When Kiviok came close to the beautiful goose girl, she trembled and looked at him in fright.

"Don't be afraid. I will help you," said Kiviok.

He quickly untied his soft fur sleeping skin and wrapped it around her trembling shoulders to give her warmth. He took her gently by the hand and led her back to his tent.

"What is your name?" asked Kiviok. And she answered, "Kungo," for she could not at first bring herself to speak with a human voice.

Kungo lived with Kiviok in his tent during the whole of the berry-picking moon and when she saw that he was good and kind, she agreed to be his wife. With the coming of the winter moon, Kungo made them both some warm new boots and clothing and sewed a new skin cover for Kiviok's kayak. When the heavy snows came and the nights were long, they made an igloo for themselves.

At last the spring sun melted their igloo, and Kungo gave Kiviok the gift of a newborn son whom they also named Kungo. At nesting time in the second spring

she gave her husband a beautiful new daughter named Kungola.

The snows of seven winters came to them and each slowly faded into summer. They lived joyfully together until one night when the thunder rumbled and the lightning flashed and the wicked raven soared over their land once more, casting a terrible spell upon the goose girl.

Next morning the snow geese flew in long V's over Kiviok's tent, sending their wild music drifting down to the earth.

"Kungo, Kungo, Kungola," they called to their beautiful sister, who was Kiviok's wife, and to her small son and daughter. "Kungo, Kungo, Kungola," they called, coaxing her to rise up with her two children and fly South with them to the unknown lands.

Kiviok saw his wife trembling with excitement and, as he looked up at the geese in the sky, he saw the wicked raven flying behind them, trying to hide himself beneath her stolen feather coat. He heard the raven calling magic words to her in a soft wooing voice as he cast his evil spell over her.

The beautiful Kungo began to scream like a wild thing. She rushed out of the tent shrieking, "Kungo, Kungo, Kungola," and, snatching up some white goose feathers from the ground, she put them between the fingers and along the arms and shoulders of her two children and placed the remaining feathers carelessly upon herself.

"Kungo, Kungo, Kungola," she cried as she waved her arms and running, tried to fly. Instantly the beautiful Kungo and her two children turned into graceful snow geese and rose into the air.

Circling round their tent, the two children, Kungo and Kungola, called, "Come with us, Father. Come with us."

Kiviok flapped his arms and tried and tried, but he could not fly.

"Farewell, farewell," the children called to him.

"Farewell, dear husband," cried his beautiful wife, as they winged away, their tears falling on him like soft rain.

Kiviok was overcome with sadness, when he saw them fly out of sight. His tent was a lonely place without his family and he scarcely ate or slept. One night when he could bear the loneliness no longer, he rolled up his warm fur sleeping skin, tied it on his back and set out at dawn toward the South, walking over the frozen mountains, searching, searching everywhere for his family. Days and nights he stumbled through the snow, hunting high and low, calling out to them, "Kungo, Kungo, Kungola."

Terrible cold came out of the North, the rocks cracked like ice crystals, huge snow slides plunged down the mountains and almost buried Kiviok. Once the wind blew so hard that he had to dig a hole in the snow and hold onto a rock with his fingers and teeth and toes to keep from being swept off a cliff. But when the wind was gone, he struggled on, calling, "Kungo, Kungo, Kungola," until his words froze and fell to the ground, shattering like icicles.

On the hundredth day of Kiviok's journey he crossed the last snow-covered mountain and started down toward the shores of the mighty sea. With each step the weather seemed to grow warmer and warmer. Five fat foxes came and ran round and round him. He caught one by the tail and ate it for his dinner. The rich food gave him new strength.

When he reached the sea, he saw the huge giant named Inukpuk whose ears were covered with hair. The giant sat carving an ivory walrus tusk. Kiviok knew that the giant was kind, so he was not afraid of him. He stood beside Inukpuk's strong right arm and watched him carve.

Each stroke of the giant's jade-green ax flung out bright chips of ivory that came to life when they fell into the sea. As they struck the water, they turned into flashing silver trout that flicked their tails and darted gracefully into the cold blue depths of the sea. Kiviok stared in wonder.

At length, Kiviok climbed up to the giant's ear, held back his hair and shouted, "Have you seen a beautiful white snow goose with two young goslings flying toward the unknown land? Please tell me, Giant, for they are my wife and children who have been enchanted by the wicked raven."

"Yes, yes. I saw them many, many days ago. They flew that way," replied the giant with a booming voice that echoed through the mountains and nearly deafened Kiviok. "They flew South," he said and pointed out across the icebergs that floated in the ocean. "They were all three crying, 'Kungo, Kungo, Kungola,' As they flew through the clouds, their tears fell on me like rain, wetting my hair."

"How can I ever reach them?" cried Kiviok. "The sea is wide and I did not bring my kayak."

"That is not so difficult," shouted Inukpuk.

The giant leaned over, put his mouth to the water, and called magic words into the sea. Big bubbles foamed around his head. Kiviok heard him shouting.

"Bubble, bubble!
A man's in trouble.
Come and help,
Oh magic fish."

He clapped his hands together and roared. "Here they come now! And look! Here comes Kakak, the father of all fish. Dive in and swim with him. He will lead you to the unknown land. He knows the way. You will be safe with him. Have a good journey," called the giant. "I hope you find your family."

Kiviok knew that this was the only way he could cross the sea, so he dove into the freezing water. The sea trout crowded all around him. He swam down into the shadowy depths, and there he found the great fish, Kakak, waiting for him.

"Climb onto my back, brother, and hold onto my fin," said Kakak. "We're on our way!"

Beneath the frozen sea they flashed all together like a flight of silver arrows. Kiviok held on, breathing air out of the magic sea bubbles. Often he thought that he would be torn from the slippery back of the fish, so he clung to Kakak's fin with all his might, as the water rushed past him. They darted past great whales and strange horned creatures that guarded dark green caves. They saw the icy, half-ruined igloos of strange sea witches almost hidden by the waving weeds that grew beneath the sea.

For many terrible days and nights they traveled through the depths of the ocean without sight of sun or moon or stars until at last they rose to the surface of the sea and Kiviok for the first time saw warm dancing waves and hot southern beaches flooded with yellow sunlight.

When they reached the shallow water, Kiviok gave his thanks to the great trout Kakak and his friends who had carried him to this place. He stood up and ran splashing through the sparkling waves onto the strange white beach. The heat of the sun was so strong that at first he thought he, himself, would melt like snow.

Kiviok searched along the shore until he found a steep mountain path that led to a narrow entrance in the cliffs. There he was stopped by the wicked raven, now grown as big as a man. The raven gave an evil laugh as he clutched poor Kungo's white feather coat beneath his claws.

Kiviok was not afraid. He spread out his arms and ran straight at the wicked raven. For one whole day they fought and wrestled until hair and feathers flew into the air.

The raven shouted, *"Cawk, cawk, cawk,"* and Kiviok shouted, "Where have you hidden my Kungo, Kungo, Kungola?"

Finally with one great heave Kiviok the Eskimo flung the wicked raven over the edge of the cliff. He splashed into the sea and was never seen again.

Kiviok snatched up the white feather coat that belonged to his beautiful wife and, looking beyond the stone entrance that the raven had guarded, he saw a lovely green valley with flowers and gentle streams that flashed gaily in the sunlight. Near the end of the valley stood a small tent just like the one he and his family had shared in the North.

Kiviok ran down into the valley. He saw his little boy, Kungo, and his daughter, Kungola, returned to human form. They ran toward him, crying out with joy, and took him by the hands and led him to the tent.

There he saw Kungo, his beautiful wife, sitting beside the entrance, plucking the last of the white feathers from her arms. Walking up to her, he shyly held out her own feather coat that he had taken from the wicked raven.

"Oh, it is good to see you," said Kungo to her husband, Kiviok. "Let us start home today, for we long to see our own land once more."

They climbed down the cliffs and when they reached the sea, Kiviok knelt on the shore, placed his lips to the water and shouted.

> *"Bubbles, bubbles!*
> *End my troubles.*
> *Help me now,*
> *Oh magic fish."*

Bubbles foamed up around Kiviok's head and with a great rush and a splash the mighty Kakak and a hundred other silver trout reappeared.

"I've found my family," shouted Kiviok, and all the trout leaped in the air for joy.

Kiviok showed his wife and children the secret way to breathe beneath the water. Then they each jumped onto the slippery back of a trout and held on tight, as they dove under the surface of the sea.

Swift as swallows they darted northward through the dark green shadows just above the ocean's floor until Kakak and the other fish flipped up out of the water and turned into sleek, ivory fish carvings that lay in a neat ring around the giant, Inukpuk.

"I'm glad to see you found your family," shouted the giant. "If only there was a river running up North, I would send you riding the rest of the way home on these magic fish of mine. Those frozen mountains you must climb will hurt the children's feet. But since there's no help for it, you will just have to start walking."

"Hear me, Giant," said Kiviok's wife. "There may be another way for us to go." And she pulled on her white feather coat and placed some wing feathers along the arms of the children.

"Kungo, Kungo, Kungola," she called. She and the children rose into the air and once more changed into three white-winged snow geese. They swooped down, and Kiviok's wife took hold of his hands; each of their children took one of his feet and they soared upward, circling around the giant's head.

"*Tugvaoteet, tugvaoteet nakoamiaseet*," they called to him in Eskimo. "Goodbye! Goodbye! Thank you very much."

"Good flying! Good landing!" shouted the giant.

Beyond the mountains they saw Kiviok's lonely footprints in the snow leading to the wide plain and the silent lake. They landed gently and laughed with joy, and all three snow geese once more became human beings.

When Kiviok put up their tent, his wife took off her goose-feather coat and said, "I shall never, never leave you again."

She whirled the magic coat around her head and flung it high in the air. It turned into the spirit of a snow goose and flew away forever.

Kiviok taught his son how to paddle their kayak and his beautiful wife taught their daughter how to sew. Some Eskimos say they are still living there today, right beside the silent lake.